HORSELAND

Horseland #5: Western Riding Winner
Copyright © 2008 DIC Entertainment Corp.
Horseland property ™ Horseland LLC
Printed in the United States of America.

Library of Congress catalog card number: 2007935201
ISBN 978-0-06-134171-7

Book design by Sean Boggs
❖
First Edition

Western Riding Winner

Adapted by
ANNIE AUERBACH
Based on the episode
"THE COMPETITION"
Written by
JAY ABRAMOWITZ

▉HarperEntertainment
An Imprint of HarperCollins Publishers

CHAPTER 1

Horseland Ranch is a very special place. Nestled in a beautiful valley, with magnificent mountains nearby, the ranch is an ideal place to ride, train, and board a horse, as well as make lifelong friends. Perhaps what makes Horseland so unique, however, is that the horses there have the ability to talk to one another—without their human riders knowing!

It's not only the horses that can talk. Even the resident cute, potbellied pig can speak . . . and sing!

"Ready?" Teeny asks. The pig jumps up on a haystack as if it were a stage. Teeny looks expectantly at her audience—Shep the Australian shepherd and Angora the cat—and then the plump pig begins her song:

> *I'm happy as a pig every day.*
> *I croon like a singer with a gig.*
> *I'll feel good tomorrow, come what may.*
> *Oh, I'm so happy to be a pig!*
> *Oink! Oink!*

The song is out of tune, but Teeny doesn't care. She jumps down and wiggles her tail so that the pink ribbon tied to it bounces. She's very proud of her performance.

"Nice one, Teeny," says Shep. The dog is known for being supportive but stern when necessary. It's his job to rule the stables, making sure all the animals keep in line. But even those in charge need to have a little fun now and then.

Shep jumps up onto the haystack and clears his throat. It's his turn to show off *his* singing voice:

> *Hey there, beasts of the field,*
> *If you see me coming,*
> *Better yield.*
> *If I say heel,*
> *Get heeled.*
> *'Cause I'm the alpha dog,*
> *And you're just a cat and a hog!*

Shep finishes the song with a great howl. Angora rolls her eyes. The gray, fluffy cat is definitely not impressed.

"Save your voice," Angora tells Shep. Then she says with a sly smile, "It's time we heard from the winner-to-be of this little singing competition: *Moi!*"

"You know, Angora," says Shep, "when you compete, winning isn't necessarily the most important thing."

Just then Sarah Whitney, one of the riders who trains at Horseland, runs over to the trio.

"Shep, I heard you howling!" exclaims the eleven-year-old girl. "I was so worried. You sounded like you were hurt!" Sarah bends over and pats the dog affectionately on the head. "Anyway, I'm glad to see you're okay."

Shep barks loudly in response.

After Sarah leaves, Angora and Teeny break into fits of giggles. They find it hilarious that Sarah mistook Shep's singing for howls of pain.

Shep shakes his head glumly. "Hurt? Only my pride, Sarah. Only my pride." He knows the others won't let him forget this anytime soon. He also knows that competition always brings out the best and the worst in both people and animals.

CHAPTER 2

Inside the stable, the riders were busy grooming their horses. Twelve-year-old Bailey Handler brushed the flank of his horse, Aztec, a strong Kiger mustang. Next to him, eleven-year-old Molly Washington was doing the same to her pride and joy, Calypso, a spotted Appaloosa. Alma Rodriguez had her nose in a book as she groomed her horse, a skewbald Pinto mare named Button. A horse lover since she was five, the now twelve-year-old girl also loved to read.

"You guys!" Alma called excitedly to the others. "This book about famous horses of the past is incredible! Did you know that a palomino stallion named Trigger was once the most famous horse in the entire country? He had a flowing white mane, and a famous cowboy rode him. In fact, they even made movies together."

Molly and Sarah looked at each other and smiled. Alma seemed to be full of facts lately.

However, not everyone was working hard. Sisters Chloe and Zoey Stilton sat on a couple of haystacks nearby. Chloe painted her nails, while Zoey brushed her long red hair. As you can imagine, the girls' laziness wasn't too popular with the other riders. But that didn't seem to bother the sisters. They believed money could buy happiness—or anything else one might need. And they certainly had plenty of money!

Just then, fourteen-year-old Will Taggert strode into the stable holding a western saddle. Besides being Bailey's cousin, Will was

the group leader when the adults weren't around and often led the riding lessons.

"I have an announcement, buckaroos," said Will.

"Buckaroos?" echoed Molly. She looked at Sarah and the two girls giggled.

Will held out the saddle and said, "I'm going to teach you cowpokes some new

9

Western riding techniques."

"All right!" cheered Sarah. She stopped grooming Scarlet, her black Arabian mare to look over at Will. "Western riding is your specialty, isn't it?" she asked.

Will blushed slightly, and he looked down at the ground. "I've done a bit," he admitted.

"*Sí, él amo* Western riding!" Alma chimed in.

Molly smirked. "Yeah, he loves Western riding . . . western omelets . . . western bar-becue . . ."

Will cut her off before she could finish. He knew Molly had a knack for being funny, but Will had a job to do. "Listen up. We're having a competition to choose one rider from Horseland to represent us at the Junior Nationals."

Molly, Alma, and Sarah looked at one another with delight. "The Junior Nationals?!" they said in unison.

Bailey stopped brushing Aztec's blue-and-brown mane and put his hands on his hips.

"Western riding is *soooo* easy," he said confidently.

Chloe and Zoey couldn't be bothered to get excited. Zoey was doing her nails now, while Chloe brushed her own long, strawberry blond hair.

Chloe sighed. "Western riding is country," she said to her sister.

Zoey agreed and made a face. "I know. Is there anything worse than country?"

"The music!" offered Chloe.

"The clothes!" added Zoey.

"Hel-*lo*! The hats!" said Chloe.

"NO!" Zoey practically screamed in horror. "Say we don't have to wear cowboy hats!" she said pleadingly to Will.

Will saw the mortified looks on the sisters' faces and just shook his head. He was used to this with the Stilton sisters.

"And what's up with those western saddles?" Chloe asked him.

"The western saddle is bigger and heavier than an English saddle," Will explained,

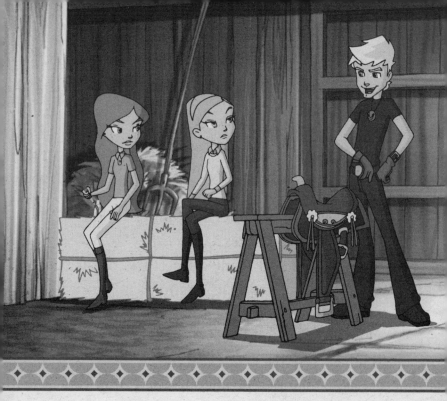

pointing to the one in front of him.

"Duh," said Chloe, rolling her eyes.

"Tell us something we *don't* know," said Zoey. She got up and went to get her English saddle. She brought it over and set it down next to Will's western saddle. "See how much lighter and smaller this English saddle is?" she asked. "Even *I* can lift it!"

"You're right, Zoey," said Will. "But the western saddle is designed for all-day-long comfort—for both horse and rider. The English saddle is designed to give the rider closer contact with the horse."

"Exactly," said Chloe, crossing her arms. "And when I ride, I need to be totally at one with my horse."

"Sure you do," Molly called out. "Until it comes time to muck out his stall!"

Even Zoey couldn't help giggling at that comment. Of course, as soon as Chloe glared at her sister, Zoey stopped laughing.

"As a matter of fact," announced Chloe, "I'm going to pass on this bogus competition altogether. I'm sticking to English riding."

"Me too!" Zoey said defiantly. "You won't see me wearing a cowboy hat over my riding helmet!"

However, the rest of the group had quite the opposite reaction to Western riding.

"I can't wait to get started!" cried Alma.

"Me too!" added Molly and Sarah.

CHAPTER 3

The next morning, the sun shone brightly in the sky, a promise of perfect riding weather. Molly, Alma, and Sarah were outside by the arena, stretching in preparation for their upcoming lesson. Bailey was relaxing on a stack of hay bales nearby, his hands behind his head. All of their horses were saddled and tethered inside the arena.

"I'm so excited, I hardly slept!" Alma gushed, as she completed a series of lunges.

"I didn't sleep much either," Sarah added, stretching up to the sky. She sighed. "But not because I'm excited."

"Something wrong, Sarah?" asked Molly, stretching to one side.

Sarah stopped stretching and looked at her friends, anxiety spreading across her face. She pushed her blond hair out of her eyes. "Yeah," she admitted. "My parents wanted me to have a new Quarter horse—the type of horse that's perfect for Western riding."

Molly furrowed her brow in confusion. "I thought you said there was something wrong."

Sarah bit her lip. "I don't want to have an unfair advantage over you three," she explained. Then she looked over at her beautiful horse. "And I love Scarlet so much. I know it's odd to say so, but I feel like I'd be betraying her."

"But, Sarah, we want you to do your best. Honest," Alma said encouragingly. "Take the horse!"

"Yeah," agreed Bailey. "Not that it'll make any difference with me and Aztec in the competition." Bailey was quite confident that he and his horse would win the Horseland competition *and* the Junior Nationals. He was already planning his acceptance speech in his head.

Meanwhile, Sarah was still unsure. "I don't know," she said reluctantly. "It doesn't feel right."

"It's only for this one competition," Molly pointed out.

Alma nodded. "Scarlet will always be your number one horse." She called over to the Arabian mare. "Right, Scarlet?"

Hmph! Scarlet thought to herself. *Easy for her to say!*

The majestic mare was visibly upset. Would she be replaced?

CHAPTER 4

Several minutes later, Will rode his palomino stallion, Jimber, into the arena. He was dressed in a Western shirt with a bolo tie around his neck. Bailey and the three girls were already on their horses, ready and excited for their first Western riding lesson. All of the horses wore western saddles that were decorated in bright colors.

Will cleared his throat. "Now, in Western, horses go at a slower gait," he began.

"Anyone know—"

"I do!" Alma interrupted, her arm raised in the air. "I read about that. It's called a 'jog.'"

"That's right," replied Will with a nod of his head. "Now, watch Jimber."

Will led his golden-colored horse to the right, and Jimber ambled along slowly. He held both reins in his right hand, his left hand relaxed at his side.

"Remember these two key things about Western," Will said to the group. "You hold both reins in one hand, and you stay behind the horse. I don't mean that literally, of course."

"I know what you mean," piped up Alma. "You teach your horse to move away from the pressure you apply."

Will nodded, impressed by Alma's knowledge. "Yup. In Western riding, there's less rein and more body. You're kind of pushing the horse in the direction you want it to go." He demonstrated what he meant by pushing his legs against Jimber's side as he lightly tugged the reins toward the right. Jimber rode in a circle, his black-streaked tail flowing behind him. The others watched intently from their horses.

"See?" Will said proudly. He and Jimber made a great team. They made it look effortless.

Then it was time for the others to try it. "Okay, your turn, Alma," said Will.

"Go, Alma!" cheered Sarah and Molly.

Alma was grateful for their support. The friends always tried to cheer one another on during lessons and competitions.

Alma's horse, Button, jogged forward, her white tail swishing behind her. Alma held the reins with one hand, but she had a hard time keeping her balance.

"Lean forward in the saddle, Alma," Will instructed.

"Caramba!" gasped Alma, wavering back and forth. She realized that it was easier to read about Western-style riding in a book than it was to perform the moves!

Sarah was next. She also found it hard to stay balanced.

"Vamanos, muchacha!" yelled Alma.

"Do it, Sarah!" shouted Molly.

Sarah wobbled, but stayed on Scarlet. She returned to the group with a smile and look of relief splashed across her face.

Molly did a better job. Just like a cowboy who needs to keep a hand free for a lasso, Molly was able to keep her free hand by her thigh and successfully steer Calypso in the direction she wanted to go.

"Beautiful, Molly!" Sarah called out.

"Great job," agreed Alma.

Molly grinned from ear to ear. She was proud of herself and her horse.

Will and Jimber rode up alongside Molly and Calypso. "Not bad for a city kid," Will told Molly. "Calypso's an Appaloosa, so she was bred for Western riding."

Molly reached out and stroked her horse's white mane. "Good girl, Calypso! The way you did that was amazing!"

Calypso whinnied happily.

At last, Bailey showed off what he and Aztec could do, completing their task with ease. Bailey felt like he was on top of the world. He turned and shouted to the others, "I told you I was meant for Western! Bring on the steers, I'm ready for some ropin'!"

But his swelled sense of pride seemed to tip his balance. Soon he was flailing around like the others. "Whoa! WHOA!" he cried.

Aztec whinnied in annoyance as Bailey almost toppled off.

23

"Sorry, Aztec!" Bailey said sheepishly, once he regained control. "I've got to get used to this."

As he turned to head back to the group, Bailey noticed that the girls couldn't hold in their giggles.

CHAPTER 5

Not long afterward, the horses were back in their stalls in the stable and had a chance to talk about the day's riding lesson.

"I can't believe I missed it!" said Chili. The gray Dutch Warmblood stallion belonged to Chloe, and they were very similar in temperament—both were unpleasant.

Aztec came to the end of his stall and leaned out, looking directly at Chili. "I'm going to say it just one more time: it was

Bailey's fault," he said in an annoyed tone. The hotheaded stallion was definitely not in the mood for Chili's snide comments.

Unfortunately, Chili didn't buy Aztec's excuse that it was Bailey's fault. He was too busy enjoying a good laugh at Aztec's expense. Chili was always happy when one of the other horses failed. Just like humans, horses could be competitive, too. And the ones at Horseland were no exception.

Sarah, Bailey, Molly, and Alma reentered the stable. Sarah could tell that Bailey was still upset about his earlier fumble.

"It doesn't mean that you failed," Sarah told him gently. "It just means you'll have to work harder at it."

"Yeah, Bailey," said Molly, walking over to them. "The way I see it, you're still the one to beat."

Bailey managed a small smile. He appre-

ciated his friends' efforts to cheer him up.

Just then, Will appeared. "Good work today, riders," he told the group, proud of the progress they had made. "See you tomorrow."

"Bye, Will," called Sarah as Will left.

"Thanks a lot," added Molly.

Alma waved. "See you tomorrow!"

Will stopped and turned around. "Oh, by the way, I just heard—Chris Alter's going to be a judge at the Junior Nationals."

"Chris Alter?!" the others cried, their eyes wide and mouths open with disbelief.

"The rock star?"

"The leader of Speedplay?"

"The singer from my favorite group?"

"The best guitar player *ever*?"

Will didn't see what all the fuss was about. "Yeah, I hear he rides a little," he explained. "See you tomorrow." He waved and headed out of the stable.

"Wait a second," Alma called, running up to him. "If I go to the Junior Nationals, will I get to, like, *meet* him?"

Will shrugged. "Yeah, I guess so." Then he turned and left.

The three girls looked at one another excitedly. "We're going to meet Chris Alter!"

28

they sang, hugging one another and jumping up and down.

Sarah pulled away. "Uh . . . wait a minute," she said, looking at her friends. "Think about it. Only *one* of us is going to meet Chris Alter."

After a moment, the girls and even Bailey enthusiastically declared, "*I'm* going to meet Chris Alter!" Their competitive spirit was about to kick into high gear.

CHAPTER 6

The following morning, Bailey, Alma, and Molly were prepping in the stable before their next lesson. All three wondered why Sarah wasn't there.

"Sarah's never late," said Alma, looking at her watch.

"I hope she's okay," Molly said nervously. She couldn't imagine what was keeping her friend, and she was a little concerned.

Just then the group heard a noise outside the stable.

"What's that?" asked Alma, as she and the others went to take a look.

Outside, a truck with a horse trailer pulled up. The trailer opened and Sarah led a beautiful, dark brown Quarter horse down the ramp. The horse was a strong and striking animal.

"What's this?" asked Molly. "A new horse?"

Sarah sighed. "My parents leased him for me on a trial basis," she explained.

Alma walked up to the horse and patted his nose. The horse whinnied. "A real Quarter horse," Alma marveled. "Bred and trained for Western riding."

"Trained for it his entire life," Sarah added. She looked down at the ground sheepishly. She felt uneasy and uncomfortable.

"Wow, Sarah! Congratulations!" Molly said, putting her hands on Sarah's shoulders. She thought Sarah was one lucky girl.

But Bailey didn't share in the excitement. He frowned and crossed his arms. "I don't know, Sarah. Maybe it *is* unfair for you to have such a big advantage in the competition," he admitted.

Sarah nodded unhappily. "Yeah, I agree."

"Come on, Bailey," Alma interjected. "Be a good sport. Can't you be happy for your friend?"

"Hey, we're talking about hanging out

with Chris Alter," Bailey reminded her, and then he turned and headed back into the stable.

Alma tucked her long brown hair behind her ears and thought about what Bailey just said. She was surprised by how she felt.

"Hmm . . . Maybe I'm not as happy for Sarah as I thought I was," she said to herself.

CHAPTER 7

Later that morning, the friends had their next Western riding lesson. When competing in Western riding, there are many different events to choose from. In the reining event, a horse and rider need to be able to complete a set pattern of maneuvers. In trail class, the rider must lead the horse through an obstacle course. Will was training the kids in both of these events.

Alma went first. Holding onto Button's reins with one hand, she rode her horse

around the large barrels placed throughout the arena. She looked uneasy, and Will could tell.

"Control, Alma!" called Will, who was sitting on Jimber. "Remember, scoring's based on smoothness, finesse, and attitude!"

Alma and Button barely made it around the next barrel. Using only one hand on the reins was more difficult than she had expected.

"Go ahead and use two hands," Will said.

"I . . . don't . . . need . . . two . . . hands," declared Alma, as she flopped around in the saddle.

"You do until you get better at this," said Will forcefully. He rode up to them, and Button slowed down. Will grabbed her reins and lead Button back to the group. "Time to take a break." He didn't want Alma or Button to get hurt.

"Wow, Alma!" said Molly with a cheeky grin. "You might not meet Chris Alter, but at least you can get a job as a circus clown!"

Alma, however, was not amused. "I'll get this down, Molly," she insisted. "And you don't have to make fun of me."

"Hey, sorry," said Molly, surprised by Alma's strong reaction. "It was just a joke."

"Look who's here!" Bailey said suddenly.

Everyone turned to see Sarah riding up on Scarlet. She looked very much at home atop the stately mare.

"Where's your new horse?" Bailey asked her.

"I just couldn't ride any horse but Scarlet," explained Sarah. She stroked Scarlet affectionately. The horse tossed her head proudly, happy to be with Sarah again.

Next, it was Molly's turn to ride the course.

"Wish me luck!" Molly called to her friends as she set out.

"Good luck!" Sarah said immediately. But Bailey stayed silent, and Alma said good luck only under her breath.

Molly and Calypso rode around and between the four barrels like a pro. Everyone watched in amazement. Will was especially impressed.

"You keep up that hard work, Molly, and

someday you may be running rings around me and Jimber," Will told her when she was finished.

Molly flashed a big smile. Then she leaned over and patted Calypso. "Did you hear that, girl? We are happenin'! We are the best!" She raised her arms in triumph.

Alma rode up next to Molly. *"Caramba!"* she exclaimed. "You sound like you already won the Junior Nationals."

Sarah rode up to the other side of Molly. "I mean, *really*. It's not over yet," Sarah said in a determined tone.

Molly looked from one girl to the other, confused by the suddenly uncomfortable atmosphere. "What's with you two, anyway?" she asked.

"Maybe our horses aren't bred to ride Western, but that doesn't mean we don't have a chance," Alma snapped.

Bailey rode up to the girls and flashed a devilish grin. "Alma, Sarah, be good sports," he mocked, imitating what Alma had said to him the previous day. "Can't you be happy for your friend?"

Sarah and Alma just glared at Bailey.

Later, inside her stall in the stable, Calypso noisily chewed some feed.

"Mmm, mmm! This feed is extra tasty today!" she announced. "Or could it be that

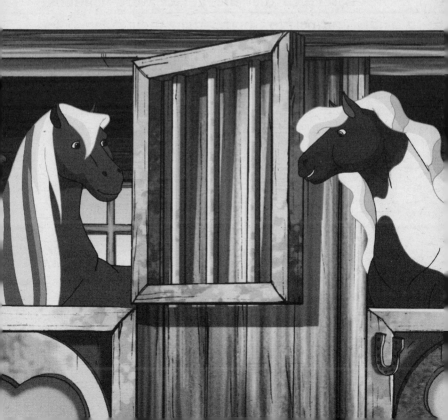

I'm just in a fantastic mood after that ride? Flawless!" She tossed her head back proudly. "I'd probably enjoy eating *rocks* right now."

Button looked over from her stall next door. "I'd be happy to get you some!" she teased.

From their stalls, Scarlet and Aztec joined in the laughter.

"Oh, you guys!" Calypso said with a smile.

It seemed that the horses were handling the competition better than their riders.

CHAPTER 8

By lunchtime, the mood between the friends had not improved. The competition was bringing out the worst side of everyone. They felt jealous, angry, and resentful. Although they sat at the same table in the cafeteria, no one talked to or looked at anyone else. The silence was painful.

"Pass the salt, please," said Alma finally, her nose buried in a book.

Bailey, who had the salt shaker in front of him, didn't respond.

"Pass the salt, PLEASE!" repeated Alma.

Bailey looked at her with surprise. "Sorry," he said and handed her the shaker.

"Thank you!" replied Alma, annoyed.

"You're welcome," Bailey answered, equally annoyed.

"You know, Alma, it's considered somewhat rude to read at the table," Sarah said.

Alma looked up from her book. "I'd tell you what I'm reading about," she began, "but you guys would just interrupt me, as usual."

Bailey crossed his arms. "I'm trying to eat, and you girls won't stop talking, 'as usual.'"

"Won't stop talking?" asked Molly. "We just started talking!"

"She's right, Bailey," said Sarah. "And I'm getting a bit tired of you putting 'us girls' down."

But Bailey wasn't about to back down.

"I'm getting 'a bit tired' of 'you girls' ganging up on me!" he said, glowering at them.

"We wouldn't have to gang up on you if you weren't so immature," replied Sarah with a huff.

"Who said *we* gang up on him?" said Alma. "*I* don't gang up on anyone."

"That's because you're not paying attention to anyone," accused Molly. "'Cause you have your nose in a book!"

"I don't always have my nose in a book!" Alma answered, defensively.

"When you're asleep, maybe," Bailey added.

Alma pursed her lips. "And if I do, maybe it's because I prefer the company of a book to some *people* I know," she pointed out.

Molly shook her head and leaned over the table. "Maybe you'd rather read because it's easier than relating to people."

"I get along great with people I *want* to get along with," Alma said, her voice beginning to rise. "What do you know about relating to people? All you ever do is tell jokes!"

Molly folded her arms. "At least I'm having fun. You're so serious all the time," she

said angrily to Alma. And with that, she stormed from the table.

Furious, the other three left the table as well. Things seemed to be going from bad to worse.

A few weeks later, the day of the competition at Horseland had finally arrived. As they prepped their horses that morning, all the riders were trying to keep focused and to remember what they had been taught during their lessons. They all kept to themselves, their friendships still strained and uncomfortable.

Soon it was time to assemble in the arena. A cool breeze swept through as Alma, Sarah, Bailey, and Molly sat astride their horses. All of the riders wore stylish cowboy hats over their helmets.

Dressed in his own Western riding gear, Will rode in on Jimber. Stopping in the center, Will addressed the group. "You guys have all worked hard for the past few weeks. And now, may the best Western rider win!"

"Or the best *dressed* Western rider," said Bailey, eyeing Sarah's expensive new hat and outfit. Around her neck was a pricey, chic yellow bolo tie.

Sarah rolled her eyes. "Grow up, Bailey," she replied, annoyed.

"'Grow up, Bailey,'" he mimicked. Then he looked her squarely in the eye and confidently said, "I'm glad you and I are doing the exact same routines, 'cause I'm going to show you how it's done."

Before Sarah could respond, Molly piped up.

"Quit arguing, you two," she said. "You're upsetting Calypso." She patted her horse's flank.

Alma pointed at Molly and said, "*You're* upsetting my stomach."

"You think you feel sick now?" Molly replied, her eyebrows raised. "Wait 'til you see me ride!"

Just then, Zoey climbed up and sat on the arena fence. No one had seen her in weeks since she had no interest in learning Western riding.

"Zoey, what are you doing here?" Will asked her.

"Just looking for entertainment," Zoey replied with a smirk. "Looks like I found it." She was hoping someone would make a mistake, and with all the arguing going on, it was likely someone would.

But Zoey was in for a surprise herself.

At that moment, Chloe arrived in the arena—riding a new horse! She was dressed in an elaborate purple-and-lilac Western jacket with white fringe on the arms and across the chest. She wore a matching cowboy hat with her helmet underneath.

"Did I miss anything?" Chloe asked.

"Only about three weeks of practice," replied Will, surprised to see her.

"Oh, don't you worry," Chloe told him. "I've been practicing a bit on my own, ever since I heard about Chris Alter. Mommy and Daddy leased this Quarter horse for me—the same one that Sarah didn't want." She looked over at Sarah and with a smirk said, "Thanks, Sarah."

Sarah grimaced, as Zoey jumped down from the fence and approached her sister. She was seething with rage, her fists clenched and eyes blazing.

"You traitor!" Zoey yelled at Chloe. "You've been working out every day? You told me you were at the library!"

"I was so amazed you believed that," Chloe replied calmly, shaking her head.

That made Zoey even madder. "Well, if you think you're going to just waltz in here and win, you've got another think coming. You know how awesome Pepper is!" Zoey fumed, hardly able to contain her anger. Being sisters didn't stop these two from arguing.

Nearby, Shep, Angora, and Teeny were watching the events unfold.

"Ooh! This is getting good!" Angora said happily. She loved drama—the more the

better. She quickly ran to the stable and up to Chili's stall. Once she made certain there were no humans around, she called to Chili.

"Chili, Chloe's entering the Western competition!" Angora revealed.

"Oh, yeah!" Chili cheered, tossing his mane. "We're going to put those losers to shame!" He was overconfident—just like his rider, Chloe.

By this point, Angora was nearly busting at the seams and couldn't wait to deliver the final blow. "Oh, and Chili? Another thing. She's riding a *new* horse."

"WHAT?!" Chili exclaimed.

Angora pranced out of the stable, pleased with herself. She was such a troublemaker— and she knew it.

CHAPTER 10

Zoey saddled Pepper in a hurry and guided her horse into the arena where everyone else was waiting. "Come on, Pepper," said Zoey, opening the stall door and guiding out her horse, a gray Dutch Warmblood mare. "Let's go show them how it's done!"

Everyone was eager to get the competition underway.

"Okay, then," began Will. "First event: the trail class. You riders will guide your horses

through the kind of obstacles you would find out on the trail."

All six riders, who were lined up at one end of the arena, were listening closely. They wanted to win the competition. They wanted to go to the Junior Nationals and meet Chris Alter. But most of all, they wanted one another to fail. The friendships had suffered terribly since the competition had begun.

"You'll be judged on the obedience of your horse and the accuracy of your form," explained Will. He looked down at his clipboard. "First up on the Horseland obstacle course will be Sarah Whitney."

Sarah urged Scarlet forward and approached a closed gate. She needed to open and close the gate, and demonstrate good form while doing it. With Scarlet facing away from the gate, Sarah leaned over, but she couldn't quite reach it. Then Scarlet moved sharply forward and threw Sarah off balance. Will scribbled a note on his clipboard.

"Ha!" Bailey scoffed.

But Sarah wasn't about to give up. She concentrated hard. Then, holding the reins in her right hand, she gave a little tug and Scarlet walked backward toward the gate. Sarah reached down and successfully opened it.

"Almost there, girl," Sarah said to Scarlet, as they walked up to the open gate. Once through, she closed the gate behind them. Sarah breathed a sigh of relief. They had done it!

Alma was next. She needed to pick up a sack filled with cans. It was easy enough—if you weren't on a horse! Riding Button, Alma approached the cans and leaned down, but she was too far from the sack to reach it. Will made more notes on his clipboard, while a disappointed Alma returned to the group.

Then Molly and Calypso got into position. They needed to go around specific markers that were set up in the arena. But they had to do it backward!

"No rush, Calypso," Molly said reassuringly to her horse. "Take your time."

Calypso backed up around the first marker . . . then the second . . . then the third! They completed the task perfectly!

"Good girl!" Molly cheered, happily giving her horse a kiss between the ears.

Will looked pleased and noted the performance.

It was Bailey's turn next. He did the same event as Sarah, but when he closed the gate, it accidentally bumped Aztec.

Then it was Chloe's chance. As she gently pressed her heels into the side of the Quarter horse, he rode forward. They approached a muddy yellow raincoat lying on the ground. Chloe bent over and successfully picked it up—while the horse was still moving. Then she put the raincoat on as they rode back to the group.

Will was impressed. "Never thought I'd see you wearing a dirty rain slicker, Chloe," he joked.

60

"Victory at any price, cowboy!" Chloe replied. She flashed a smug grin at her sister, who was up next.

"Come on, Pepper!" Zoey said. "Let's show 'em!"

The horse whinnied in reply and strode forward. When she came to an L-shaped course in the arena, Zoey said, "Turn, Pepper."

The horse turned around, her back to the course. But when Zoey instructed her to walk backward, the horse didn't know what she meant.

"Come on, Pepper," pleaded Zoey. "You're embarrassing me!" She pulled hard on the reins.

Will immediately rode over. "Zoey, you can't expect a horse to do something she's not trained to do—especially when you haven't practiced!" he told her firmly. Then he reached over and stroked Pepper. "It's okay, girl. Good job."

Zoey was furious. In a huff, she rode straight over to Chloe. "This is all your fault," she accused. "And now I have this, like, humongous blister on my hand. It hurts so much, I can't even finish the competition!" she moaned.

Chloe reached for Zoey's hand. "Oh, poor Zoey. Let me see your big bad boo-boo—*that you don't even have!*" Zoey's hand was unblemished!

Zoey pulled her hand away. "It's under the skin," she declared. "And it hurts!" She glared at Chloe. "You knew I'd beat you if I practiced, so you worked out behind my back!"

Chloe gave a small wicked smile. "Get real, little sister. You couldn't beat me if you practiced for a year."

Zoey put her hands on her hips. "Oh yeah?" she fumed. "Well, I want back that Chris Alter CD that I loaned you."

Chloe folded her arms. "And you can give me back my Chris Alter T-shirt the second we get home!" she insisted.

"If *you're* going to be there, then I'm not going home!" Zoey proclaimed.

Nearby, Sarah watched the sisters argue. *They're so horrible to each other,* she thought. Then she looked at the other riders and wondered, was the competition more important than their friendship?

CHAPTER 11

Tension was high and tempers were flaring as Will began the next phase of the competition: reining.

"Let's go, Aztec," Bailey said to his horse.

As they headed toward the starting point, Sarah rode up on Scarlet.

"Bailey, wait!" she called.

"What are you trying to do? Distract me?" Bailey said.

"No," Sarah replied. She swallowed hard. "I want to wish you the best of luck."

Bailey looked at her in surprise.

Sarah continued. "And to remind you to keep your free hand down by your side. I noticed you've been lifting it in practice lately."

Bailey was suspicious. "What are you trying to pull, Sarah?" he asked. Her heartfelt demeanor was the last thing he expected.

"It was really awful watching Chloe and Zoey treat each other with such disrespect," Sarah explained. "Then I realized something: *We've* been behaving the same way!"

Molly and Alma glanced at each other. Was Sarah right?

"We've put winning before our friendship," Sarah continued. "And I, for one, am going to stop doing that right now." She smiled. "I love you like my own sisters . . . and brother. And no riding competition or rock star is going to change that. *Ever.*"

The others were impressed by Sarah's impassioned speech. They all felt ashamed and embarrassed by their behavior.

"You're right, Sarah," said Molly. "I can't believe we let it get to this. Our friendship is way more important than winning."

"Even if meeting Chris Alter *is* the prize," added Alma, softening.

Molly turned to Alma and grabbed her hands. "I'm so sorry I said those things to you."

Alma shook her head. "It's okay. I was worse!" she said regretfully.

Just then Chloe rode over and interrupted. "So, are you kids giving up? You might as well, you know," she said smugly.

"*No one's* giving up," Sarah said pointedly.

Bailey, Alma, and Molly heartily agreed. Despite all that had happened, the friends were determined to finish.

So the competition continued.

As Bailey led Aztec in circles, he kept his free hand at his side, just as Sarah had advised. His friends cheered him on from the sidelines.

"Beautiful, Bailey!" shouted Sarah.

68

"Way to go!" Molly said.

"Keep it up!" called Alma, encouragingly. *"Andale!"*

When it was Molly's turn, she and Calypso needed to do a difficult move called a rollback. The pair rode to one end of the arena at full speed, and then, in one continuous motion, they quickly turned and galloped back in the opposite direction. Molly and Calypso did it again on the other side of the arena, and Molly beamed with pride as she tipped her hat. Sarah, Alma, and Bailey whooped and hollered with excitement at Molly's success.

Then, after Alma and Chloe completed their tasks, the group assembled by the arena gate, eager to hear the final results. They chatted excitedly. Who would win the competition? Who would go to the Junior Nationals? And who would get the chance to meet Chris Alter?

Will rode over to the group. "Okay, quiet down if you want to find out who's going to the Junior Nationals," he said. He looked down at his clipboard and then up at the expectant faces staring back at him. "And the winner is, thanks to her impeccable and most unexpected performance . . . Chloe Stilton!"

"Woo-hoo! Yes!" exclaimed Chloe. She

jubilantly punched her fist into the air.

"Way to go, Chloe!" said Sarah, support-ively. She knew Chloe deserved to win because she had done the best job, even if she didn't have the best personality.

"You were fantastic!" Alma told Chloe.

The group gave Chloe a round of applause. She felt on top of the world. But before she knew it, Alma, Bailey, Sarah, and Molly were gone! Chloe was all alone in the arena.

Hey, where'd everybody go? Chloe won-dered, her smile fading away. Now there was no one to celebrate her victory with.

The other riders had tethered their horses and were already walking together out of the arena.

"What do you say we grab my new CD player and listen to some hot Chris Alter CDs?" Sarah suggested to her friends.

"We may as well," said Molly. "That's probably the closest we're ever going to be to him!"

Everyone laughed as they linked arms. It was true that their chance to meet Chris Alter had passed, but they didn't mind so much now that their friendships were back intact.

CHAPTER 12

A week later, the friends were busy working in the stable. Bailey and Molly were grooming their horses, Alma was mucking out Button's stall, and Sarah was sweeping in front of Scarlet's stall.

Suddenly, Chloe walked in, wearing her best Western riding clothes.

"Chloe!" Alma cried. She dropped the pitchfork she was holding and ran over to her.

Bailey, Molly, and Sarah also ran over, eager

to hear the news from the competition.

"How'd the Junior Nationals go?" Molly asked excitedly.

"I lost," Chloe admitted, looking at the ground.

"Oh, Chloe, I'm so sorry," Sarah said sympathetically, putting her hand on Chloe's shoulder.

Molly hesitated a moment and then smiled slyly. "But what we *really* want to know is—"

"Did you get to meet Chris Alter?" interrupted Alma, almost dying of anticipation. "What was he like?" Her eyes were wide and hopeful.

"Oh my gosh, what a huge letdown," Chloe replied, shaking her head.

The others were surprised. Chris Alter a letdown? How could that be? The friends were anxious for Chloe to explain.

"First, his girlfriend was there. And they were both *old*! He was at least *thirty*!" said Chloe, shocked and horrified. "And then, in honor of the Western competition, he played a *country* song! It was hideous!" She scrunched up her face as if she had just eaten a sour pickle.

Alma was confused. "What are you talking about?"

"Dudette, we *love* country now!" Bailey explained to Chloe with a thumbs-up.

Sarah nodded happily in agreement. "Hey! Let's break out the CDs!" she said.

"Nooooo!" Chloe cried and ran right out of the stable. No more country *anything* for her!

CHAPTER 13

After overhearing Chloe tell her news to the other riders, Shep, Teeny, and Angora stroll into the stable.

Shep turns to Angora and says, "I think Chloe likes country music about as much as you like hairballs."

"Well, I do hate hairballs," Angora replies. "But I just *love* country music!" She jumps up on a nearby bale of hay, eager to show off her singing voice. "Listen to this!"

*"I'm as lonely as a stallion, without a mare.
Lonely as a rabbit, without a hare.
Lonely as a table, without a chair . . ."*

Unfortunately, everyone else's ears are lonely for some singing that's in tune! Angora's high-pitched voice sounds awful.

"You know, Shep," Teeny says to the dog, "I love country music, but what Angora's doing isn't music!"

"You're right!" agrees Shep. Without wasting another minute, he turns and runs right out of the stable.

Angora doesn't seem to notice. She just keeps screeching out of tune.

"Oh, no, no, no! Not good!" cries Teeny. "Hurts my ears!" The pig turns tail and follows Shep out and away from the "singing."

But that still doesn't stop Angora. Her song continues:

"I just can't take it anymore . . ."

"Neither can we!" declares Aztec from his stall.

"Somebody get that cat to a vet!" says Calypso. She wishes she could cover her ears. The horrible shrieking startles all of the other horses. Why would an animal make such dreadful sounds on purpose? It's doubtful there will be another singing competition any time soon—unless it's for the worst singer at Horseland!

Meet the Riders and Their Horses

Sarah Whitney is a natural when it comes to horses. Sarah's horse, **Scarlet,** is a black Arabian mare.

Alma Rodriguez is confident and hard-working. Alma's horse, **Button,** is a skewbald pinto mare.

82

Molly Washington has a great sense of humor and doesn't take anything seriously—except her riding. Molly's horse, **Calypso,** is a spotted Appaloosa mare.

Chloe Stilton is often forceful and very competitive, even with her sister, Zoey. Chloe's horse, **Chili,** is a gray Dutch Warmblood stallion.

Zoey Stilton
is Chloe's sister. She's also very competitive and spoiled. Zoey's horse, **Pepper,** is a gray Dutch Warmblood mare.

Bailey Handler
likes to take chances. His parents own Horseland Ranch. Bailey's horse, **Aztec,** is a Kiger mustang stallion.

Will Taggert is Bailey's cousin and has lived with the family since he was little. Because he's the oldest, Will is in charge when the adults aren't around. Will's horse, **Jimber,** is a palomino stallion.

85

Spotlight on Quarter Horses

Breed: Quarter horse

Physical Characteristics:
- Muscular
- Compact body
- Short head
- Strong, powerful hindquarters

Personality:
- Calm
- Steady
- Versatile
- Gentle

Fun facts:
- The Quarter horse got its name because of its amazing speed running a quarter of a mile.
- There are two types of Quarter horses: Standard and Running.

- They are used not only on cattle ranches, but also for mounted police units.
- The Quarter horse's compact body is perfect for the intricate maneuvers performed in Western riding events.
- The Quarter horse is the most populous horse breed in the United States. There are more than 2 million in the United States alone.

87

Chloe's Training Tips for a Reining Competition

Competing at horse shows and rodeos can be a highlight for Western riders. The reining portion of a Western riding competition requires the rider and horse to perform a specific pattern of circles, spins, and stops. Here are some great hints and explanations to help you train properly for this event.

Circles

The horse rides in larger circles at a faster speed and smaller circles at a lope.

Training Tips:

-  Make sure all the circles are perfectly round.
- Remember, it is up to the rider to determine the pace of the horse.

Backup

The horse backs up for at least ten feet.

Training Tips:

- Make sure your horse moves in a straight line.
- Don't forget to pause a moment before the next movement.

Sliding Stop

The horse goes from a gallop to a complete halt, allowing its hind feet to slide.

Training Tip:

- Make sure not to pull on the reins.

Rollback

*Following a sliding stop, the horse makes a
180-degree turn.*

Training Tip:

 Remember, there should be no pause between a
sliding stop and a rollback.

Rundown

*The horse gallops at least twenty feet
from the fence of the arena.*

Training Tip:

 Remember that it's up to the rider to maintain
control and determine the speed.

Spins

*The horse does a series of turns
in place around its inside leg.*

Training Tip:

 Make sure your horse's hindquarters stay in the
same position throughout the spin.

Hesitate

The horse must demonstrate the ability to stand still at a particular point in the riding pattern.

Training Tip:

 Make sure your horse is relaxed for this move.

Flying Change

The horse changes its leading front and hind legs mid-stride without breaking gait.

Training Tip:

 Make sure your horse doesn't change speed during this maneuver.

CHECK OUT THE NEXT ADVENTURE IN HORSELAND™!

Based on the CBS Saturday morning animated show *Horseland*.

Join Alma as she learns how to navigate the rocky road of dealing with a first crush. With the help of her friends and a quick makeover, Alma ditches the tomboy look. Will this give her the courage to finally talk to the boy she likes?

READ ABOUT ALL OF YOUR FAVORITE CHARACTERS AT HORSELAND RANCH

📚 HarperEntertainment
An Imprint of HarperCollins*Publishers*

WWW.HARPERCOLLINSCHILDRENS.COM